SPOTS ARE SPECIAL!

SPOTS ARE SPECIAL!

Kathryn Osebold Galbraith

PICTURES BY

Diane Dawson

Atheneum   1976   New York

A MARGARET K. MCELDERRY BOOK

Library of Congress Cataloging in Publication Data

Galbraith, Kathryn Osebold.   Spots are special!
"A Margaret K. McElderry book."
Summary: Having chicken pox provides a little girl
with a chance to make up all sorts of games.
(1. Play—Fiction) I. Dawson, Diane. II. Title.
PZ7.G1303Sp   (E)   75-28179   ISBN 0-689-50038-6

Published simultaneously in Canada by
McClelland & Stewart, Ltd.
Manufactured in the United States of America
Printed by Halliday Lithograph Corporation
West Hanover, Massachusetts
Bound by A. Horowitz & Son/Bookbinders
Fairfield, New Jersey
First Edition

To Steve

It was Eric who saw it first.

"Hey, Sandy. What's that on your neck?"

"Where?" asked Sandy, trying to stretch her neck enough to peer under her chin.

"There," said her brother, and he pointed to a small reddish rash just above her collar.

Mother came over and looked at Sandy's neck and chest. She laid a cool hand on Sandy's warm forehead.

"Well," said Mother, "I'm not surprised. Lots of children in your school have the chicken pox, and it looks like you have them too. You'd better stay away from her, Eric. I don't want both of you sick."

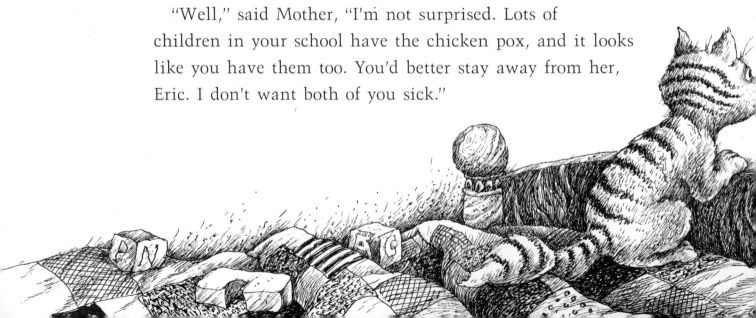

By the next morning Sandy's rash had spread to her face. She didn't feel sick, but her spots were beginning to itch.

"Boy, do you ever look funny," teased Eric when he peeked into her room on his way to school.

Sandy made a face at him. "You're just jealous because
you don't have any spots."

"What do I want with spots? I don't want to look
like *that*." He pointed a finger at her and laughed.

"You'll be sorry," she called after him. "Spots are special."

It was almost suppertime when Eric came home after school that day. He stopped at Sandy's bedroom door.

She was perched on the top of her small table. As soon as she saw Eric, she drew back her lips and snarled. She swiped at the air with her hand and hissed.

"Hey, what are you playing?"

"I'm a great fierce leopard in her tree," she said. Then
she climbed down on her hands and knees and padded
over to her bed, flicking her green bathrobe belt-tail. She
ducked under the bed so that all Eric could see were
two brown eyes peering out from under the blue bedspread.
"Now I'm back in my cave," she said and snarled again.

"That's pretty neat," said Eric. He dropped down on his
hands and knees, too. Lifting his head, he let out a roar.

"No, you can't play," said Sandy firmly. "You don't
have any spots. Only people with real spots can be
leopards." Sandy snarled and growled ferociously and then
disappeared under the bed.

The next afternoon, after Eric had a snack, he went to Sandy's room. She was crouched down in the middle of the rug on the floor. "Crrr-oak," she croaked, when she saw her brother, and gave a great leap toward him.

"Hey, what are you playing?" asked Eric.

"I'm a green spotted frog," said Sandy, "and I'm hunting for my dinner." She leaped up in the air and came down smacking her lips. "Crr-oak. I love fat flies."

Eric squatted down and hopped three times. "We can have a frog leaping contest," he said.

"No," said Sandy. "You can't play. You don't have any spots. Only people with real spots can be frogs."

That night, right after supper, Eric's first stop was
Sandy's room. Sandy was curled up on top of her bed.
Suddenly she cocked her head, listened, and then shouted,
"Fire!" Climbing off her bed, she began to crawl around
the room as fast as she could, barking wildly as she went.

"Hey, what are you playing?"

"I'm a Dalmatian, silly," said Sandy, pausing near the door. "I'm chasing the fire engines. Good-bye!" And off she hurried.

"Ding, ding, ding. Make way for the fire engines," cried Eric. He began to wail like a siren.

"No," shouted Sandy. "You can't play. You don't have any spots. Only people with real spots can be Dalmatians. Besides, the fire is out now, and I'm going to sleep until the next one." She crawled back up on her bed and closed her eyes.

The next afternoon Eric raced home to Sandy's room. Sandy was on her hands and knees with a bowl of pretzels on the floor in front of her. Her arms were spread very far apart, and she had to lean way over to reach the food with her mouth without bending her elbows.

"Hey, what are you playing?" asked Eric eagerly.

"I'm a giraffe," said Sandy. "My neck is so long I have to spread my front feet to reach the ground." Carefully she lowered her head again and crunched on a pretzel.

Eric stood on his tiptoes and tried to nibble the shade
of Sandy's tall dresser lamp.

"You can't play, Eric," said Sandy. "You don't have any
spots. Only people with real spots can be giraffes."

The next day was Saturday and Sandy slept late.
Suddenly her bedroom door was flung open and Eric came
bursting in. He was chewing on his brown corduroy
slipper, growling and snarling and shaking his head from
side to side.

"You can't be a leopard," cried Sandy. "You don't have
any...ohhhh!"

That day there was a pack of leopards in Sandy's room,

then a pond full of frogs,

a herd of giraffes,

and a firehouse full of Dalmatians.

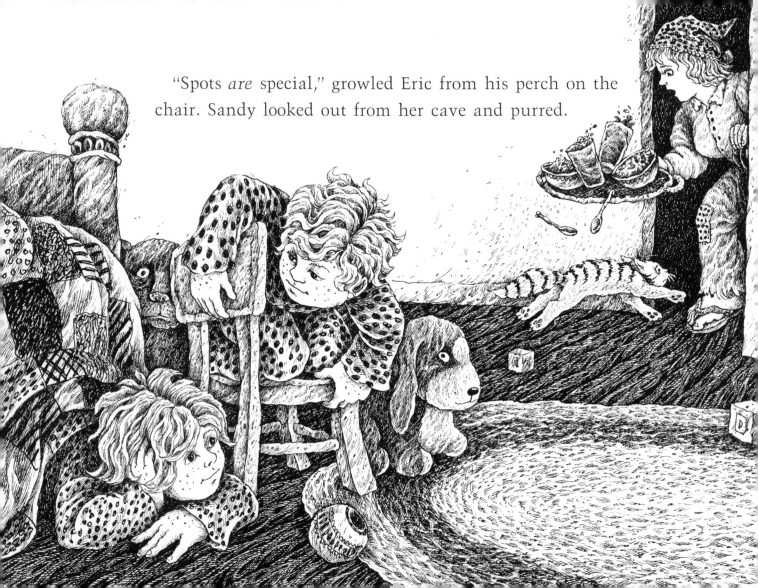

"Spots *are* special," growled Eric from his perch on the chair. Sandy looked out from her cave and purred.